of the

The Secret of the
Brownstone House

The Secret of the Brownstone House

NORAH SMARIDGE

Illustrated by Michael Hampshire

DODD, MEAD & COMPANY

NEW YORK

For JANET CAMPBELL FOX
who is young in heart

1   2   3   4   5   6   7   8   9   10

Library of Congress Cataloging in Publication Data

Smaridge, Norah.
The secret of the brownstone house.

SUMMARY: When Robin tries to unlock the
secret of the brownstone house, her New York City
visit takes an unexpected turn.
[1. New York (City)—Fiction.
2. Runaways—Fiction] I. Hampshire, Michael A. II. Title.
PZ7.S6392Se   [Fic]   77-6504
ISBN 0-396-07474-X

1

"You two will have to come up with something—and fast," Robin's father said. He left the room, letting the door bang. Then he opened it again. "What's the matter with camp, anyway?"

"Everything," Robin said. "Watery cabbage for supper. Bugs in the beds. And all that singing around the campfire." She eyed her father coldly. "I'm too old for summer camp."

"No, you're not," her mother said. She waited until Robin's father had gone. "And you don't have to go to Camp Indian Head if you think you're too old for it. You can go to music camp—or riding camp."

"Or a camp for fat girls," Robin said. Her new bra had a B cup, how about *that*? "I keep telling you, Mother. I want to go to France with you and Daddy!"

"And I keep telling you that's *out*, dear." Her mother sounded tired. This had been going on for days. "Whatever would you find to do on an

5

art tour? Daddy and I will be looking at pictures all day."

"I'd find plenty to do," Robin said. "I'd wait for you in one of those sidewalk eating places. Eat frogs, and watch the people." Too bad I can't speak French, she thought. I'd pick up a French boy and let him kiss my hand. A French boy would be fun after American kids—like that clown who lived next door, Buzz.

Her mother was thinking hard. "I know!" she said. "Why not stay with Aunt Doll in the country? She'd love to have you."

"You can say that again," Robin said darkly. "She'd get a sitter for nothing, wouldn't she?" Aunt Doll, her father's sister, had just had another baby.

"*Robin!*" Her mother was mad now. She had a right to be. Aunt Doll was always sweet to Robin. She sent her such nice things on her birthday. That beautiful rain hat—and her "mood" ring. The ring turned blue when she was feeling happy and brown when she was down. And bright red when she bumped into that new teacher. He was so good-looking that the girls were all in love with him.

"You'll have to think of something without me," Mrs. Green said. "I've got to see about supper." At the door she called back, "And you'd better keep out of your father's way. He isn't liking you very much right now."

That makes two of you, Robin thought. All you want is each other. They were going to see old pictures, were they? That's what they called it, but she knew better! It was one of those second honeymoon deals. At their age!

Second honeymoon or not, she was going with them. Oh, she'd give them a break. Keep out of their way. Why couldn't she pick up two or three French boys, not just one. They could show her Paris. Not old buildings, or parks. They could do *fun* things, like walking under the city in those sewers.

She went to her bedroom and put on her new pants. They were the color of her eyes, kind of green-blue. And wow, were they skinny! She began walking around the room with a wiggle.

7

Not bad. Those French boys would think she was sixteen. Fifteen, anyway.

She looked at her watch. There was time to see Bunny before supper. Bunny was her best friend, and part French. She'd get Bunny to teach her how to say, "You're the first French boy I've ever met." Or, "Why don't we have something to drink?" Even little children drank wine in France, she had heard.

On her way out, she saw her mother in the living room, on the phone. Her voice was oh-so-surprised, like when Daddy brought her flowers or one of those crazy pictures she liked so much.

"It's wonderful to talk to you after all these years," Mrs. Green was saying. "I can't believe you're really a judge! A lawyer, yes—but a *judge*—"

Robin moved closer. The door was open so it didn't matter if she listened. She wanted to hear more about this judge. He must be one of Mother's old boy friends. (What a good thing Mother had picked Daddy! Think of having a judge for a father).

But what did he want with Mother? Daddy

wouldn't let him come near her. Daddy was still in love with Mother. Well, she *was* good-looking—for a woman her age. She even looked right in a jumpsuit. Not like Bunny's mother who was as big as an elephant.

Robin started as she heard her own name. "Oh, Robin's a dear child. Very bright—and pretty, too. Right now, though, she's a bit hard to please." She dropped her voice but it wasn't hard to guess what she was talking about.

"You really mean that? You're *sure*?" Mrs. Green's voice rose again. "I can't even begin to tell you what it would mean to Will and me!" She laughed. "And if anyone could keep Robin in line, *you* could. You must meet with all kinds of young people in your work—girls and boys who take dope—"

Robin missed the rest of it. She was standing quite still, cold all over. And her mood ring had turned *black*. Whatever was Mother saying? "If anyone could keep Robin in line." She wasn't *out* of line, was she? She hadn't done anything—only wanted to go to France.

"Oh, Robin, there you are!" Mrs. Green came

out of the living room, smiling. "Wait till you hear this! Everything's turning out just fine. While Daddy and I are in France, you're going to stay in New York City! *New York City,* Robin." She said it as if it were heaven.

"Not with any judge, I'm not," Robin said loudly. "If you think you can just pack me off to some old boy friend of yours, you'd better think again. I've never even *met* him!"

Mrs. Green laughed. "Honey, I was talking with Ann Fox. You must have heard me speak of Ann! She and I were friends in high school and we've written to each other every New Year since then."

"Oh, *her,*" Robin said. "I remember, sort of."

"Ann's a judge now! She wanted us both to come and visit her, you and me. Then, when I told her I was going to France with Daddy, she said she'd love to have *you* to stay."

A woman judge. That could be even worse, Robin thought. Men were soft, like boys. Most of the time it was easy for a girl to get around them. But women could be hard as nails. She'd guess that this Judge Fox was a Women's Libber, too.

Not wearing a bra, or getting her hair done. And always wanting to do a man's work—like being a judge.

"You'll be on your own when Ann's in court," her mother told her. "But there's plenty to do in New York City. Open air plays in the park. Horses, if you want to ride. Indoor swimming pools—" She stopped. "Robin, where are you going?"

"To look for Daddy and tell him," Robin called back. "He won't make me go and stay with some old woman judge!" But she slowed a little. Come to think of it, Daddy wouldn't be much help. He almost always did what Mother wanted him to do.

2

Just as she thought he would, Robin's father sided with her mother. "You'll have much more fun in New York than you would with us," he said. "No pretty girl wants to look at old pictures all day." He had his arm around her and he was liking her again. "How long has your friend Ann lived in the city, dear?" he asked his wife.

"Oh, years," Mrs. Green told him. "By now she must know it like the back of her hand. And I'm sure she'll know some nice girls for Robin to run around with."

"Who needs *girls*?" Robin's father said. "Robin likes boys—and boys like Robin."

Mrs. Green smiled. "Well, there seems to be a Ricky living across the hall from Ann. Or maybe it's Micky. I couldn't hear very well. There was a noise on the line. Anyway, Ann said something about Robin having fun with Ricky—"

"Or was it Micky?" Robin said coldly. Inside,

12

though, she was pleased. Things were looking up. But it would help to know if the boy was called Ricky or Micky.

Ricky sounded Italian, and Italian boys were old for their years, like French boys. Bunny's cousin, Kay, had an Italian boy friend. He was seventeen, but he could pass for twenty. And did, sometimes. He was always giving Kay things. Like a real gold ring and one of those big blow-yourself-up pictures of himself. Kay had to hide it from her mother.

But if the boy was Micky, he'd be Irish. Robin smiled. Irish boys could be cut-ups. Like Pat. She often wished that Pat were her boy friend, but he belonged to her friend Kitten. Pat smoked pot and was always sleepy in class. But even the terrible Miss Miles, their English teacher, said that Pat could charm the birds off the trees.

"Dreaming, Robin?" Her father's voice made her jump. "Let's go have supper. I'm hungry." While they were eating, he looked at her with love. "Are you feeling better about things now, honey?"

13

"I don't know," Robin said. Which wasn't quite true. She *did* feel better. She was even eating fish, which she hated.

Later that week, Mom took her shopping for clothes. "Not only pants," Mom said. "And by the way, no bare feet in New York, not even in the apartment."

They went to Pretty Please. Mom loved their things. Miss Cash waited on them. 'I've been wishing you would drop in," she told Mrs. Green. "I have a dream of a dress in your color."

"Thanks, but it will have to stay a dream. We're shopping for Robin today. She's going to visit in New York for six weeks."

"Oh, wonderful. She'll have a ball," Miss Cash said. She turned to Robin. "You know what they call New York? Fun City." She looked Robin up and down. "You're filling out. You'll take an eight, I think. Shall we start with a suit? Then some pretty sweaters to go with it. And maybe a little number to wear when you have dinner out. And then—"

"And then we'll stop, if not before," Mrs.

14

Green said. "The suit, yes. But I think she has enough sweaters. Maybe one nice shirt."

Robin wasn't listening. She was thinking about dinners out. She pictured a beautiful eating place, with pink lights and with fresh flowers on the tables. And music, of course. Ricky would sing softly to it . . .

But if he were *Micky,* what then? Micky didn't fit the picture. He belonged with hot dogs. Or one of those places where you could fill up on meat and beer. Robin made a face. She had tried beer once. Never again!

They looked at lots of things and Robin liked most of them. At last they bought a white suit. ("But do watch that catsup you pour over everything!" her mother said.) Robin picked out a shirt that Miss Cash called "quite funny." "It's a city print," she said. "Something new. Look at those buildings and parks, and all those little cars!"

But Mrs. Green put her foot down when Robin wanted the gold dress. "*Much* too old for you," she said. "It makes you look like a pop singer!"

"What's wrong with that?" Robin wanted to

know. But Miss Cash sided with her mother and Robin had to take a pink dress. "She looks just as sweet as she can be!" Miss Cash cried. "A real picture."

"I wish the price were sweeter," Mrs. Green said. But she smiled. "Oh, well, she'll be able to wear it to parties next winter."

Would Ricky think she was a picture, Robin wondered. And if he were Micky—well, somehow she didn't think Micky would care what a girl wore. He might get a smile out of that city print thing, though.

When they got home, Robin gave a dress show for her father. He looked at her as if he couldn't believe his eyes. He was used to seeing her always in pants. "She's a young lady now," he said in a funny voice. "And I don't think I like it."

Well, *I* do, Robin thought. She took her new clothes up to her room and put them away carefully. Not just throwing them over a chair.

That night she lay awake for a long time, thinking of Fun City and what she would do there. Somehow it made her hungry. Sliding out of bed, she started for the kitchen. As she passed her parents' room the door was open and she could hear them talking. Daddy sounded uptight. "I wish she wasn't going to New York," he said. "She's so young—and so pretty. When you read about all the things that happen in that city—"

"Don't, dear," his wife said. "Robin will be quite safe with Ann. She won't let her go around alone where there's any danger. And Robin knows how to take care of herself—"

"I wonder," her father said. "The trouble is, that child's not afraid of anything or anyone. Maybe we'd better take her with us, after all? It's not too late."

Robin went back to her room. She wasn't hungry any more. She'd just *die* if she couldn't go to New York. Now that she had all those new clothes. And with Ricky there!

3

Robin's mother got her way. For once, Robin was glad of it. The next day, her father brought home her air ticket. He tried to look pleased about it but was not quite happy.

"I've spoken to the bank about traveler's checks for you, so go down and get them," he said. "You'll have to sign your name ten times! I hope one hundred will be enough."

"One hundred!" Robin said. "Why, that's a fortune, Daddy!"

"Not in New York," her mother said. "Fares and shows—and you'll want to get a gift for Bunny. But don't carry much cash around with you. New York's full of pickpockets."

"They won't get a cent from me," Robin promised. She didn't know how she could thank Daddy enough. She'd bring him something nice from New York. Maybe a pipe. He'd look fine with a pipe.

A few days later, her mother drove her to the plane. She told the stewardess that Robin was

18

flying alone for the first time. "She'll be met at the airport, but what does she do if our friend is late or anything?"

"We'll keep an eye on her." The stewardess smiled. She was used to jumpy mothers. "Let's see if we can find someone nice for her to sit with."

She passed up three women. An old lady, talking to herself. A young woman with a noisy little boy. And a woman who looked like a teacher.

Then she stopped near a nun. A young, smiling one—but a *nun.* I've never spoken to a nun in my life, Robin thought. Whatever can I talk about?

But the stewardess only bent down to the nun. "Say a little prayer for me, Sister," she said with a smile. And moved on, to a seat next to a good-looking man. Not as old as Daddy, Robin thought, but not young.

"Hi there, Mr. Hill," the stewardess said. "I have someone nice to sit with you." To Robin she said, "Mr. Hill often flies with us."

"Happy to meet you, Miss —"

"Green. Robin Green." Robin gave him her movie-star smile.

"Miss Green. I'll start by letting you have the window seat." He looked at the stewardess. "I must say that this looks much better than my last flight. You sat me next to a woman with a baby. A very wet baby—and she dumped it on my lap when she went to speak to a friend."

The stewardess laughed. "You'll note I'm not seating Miss Green on your lap!" Someone called to her, and she went off.

For Robin, the flight was fun. They had lunch soon after take-off. Mr. Hill gave her his salad in return for her cake. "Rabbit food," he said. "I always think there are bugs in it."

Robin laughed. "Not the way my mother washes greens!"

Mr. Hill took a nap after lunch. "Shake me if I snore," he said. Robin was too wide awake to nap. For a time, she looked out at the sky. Then she read a bit. Then she just sat back and thought about Ricky-Micky.

When Mr. Hill woke up, they talked for a long time. She told him about her father and mother going to France, and he told her he was a lawyer and got about a lot.

20

"A lawyer?" Robin said. "Then maybe you know Mother's friend, the one I'll be staying with? Judge Fox."

Mr. Hill smiled. "Everyone knows of Judge Fox. She's in the Children's Court, and a very fine judge. I don't know her to talk to but I've seen her often."

"What does she look like?"

He thought a minute. "Like a nice little bird. Brown hair, dark eyes, and a quick smile."

"Thanks," Robin said. "Now it should be easy to pick her out."

After a while, she told him about Ricky-Micky. "I think I like Micky better," Mr. Hill said. "He sounds fun, but maybe a little on the wild side. On the other hand, Ricky might know his way around the city better."

Just before landing, Mr. Hill took out a card and handed it to Robin with a bow. "Here's my card," he said. "Have a great time in Fun City, and call me if you need me."

Robin laughed. "I don't really expect to get into trouble with the law," she said. "But you never know." She put the card away carefully. It

21

would be something to show Bunny when she got home.

Thanks to what Mr. Hill had told her, she was able to pick out Judge Fox quickly. Small, dark, nice-looking, in a soft gray suit, and hatless. "Judge Fox," Robin said. "I'm Robin. It's so nice of you to ask me to stay."

"I'm very happy you liked the idea of coming," Judge Fox said. "But do call me Ann—it makes me feel younger." She picked up Robin's suitcase. "How was your flight?" She made a funny face. "I always try to duck flying—I can never understand what makes that huge thing stay *up*." She led the way to the parking lot. "Here's my car—hop in."

On the way to the city, she told Robin about her housekeeper, May Childs. "She comes three or four times a week, but she'll come every day while you're here. She'll be so happy to have someone in the apartment. It's lonely for her, with me out so much. She tells me she keeps the TV on, just to hear voices."

"Has she far to come?" Robin wanted to know.

"About half an hour. She lives with her son on

the West Side. She has four daughters and goodness knows how many grandchildren." Judge Fox smiled. "I hope they didn't feed you too well on the plane. May loves cooking—she'll have made enough for an army. Chicken, cherry pie —"

"I'm always hungry," Robin said. Her mouth began to water. Cherry pie was something she could never get enough of, especially the kind made with cream cheese.

After a long drive, they stopped in front of a small apartment house on East 89th Street. "Here we are, and it's one floor up," Judge Fox said.

Robin took her suitcase out of the back seat.

"Go on in. I'm sure May has the door open." Judge Fox smiled. "I'll put the car away and be with you in a few minutes."

In a doorway marked 2B stood a thin, smiling woman in a flowered dress. She held out her hand. "So you're Robin," she said. "I'm very glad to see you. It'll be so good to have someone young and pretty around the place. Not that the Judge isn't real nice-looking," she added quickly.

4

Robin followed May to the room that was to be
hers. A back room, smaller than her room at
home, but pretty. Green and white, with a white
writing table, a low armchair, and a bed with a
soft green cover. On the bed were two toy dogs.
"The Judge thought you'd like some friends."
May laughed. "She's had those dogs since she
was a little girl." She pointed to the table near
the bed. "The flowers are from the Judge but the
candy is from me."

"Oh, May, thank you," Robin said. Candy
made you fat, but it *was* nice to have by you if you
woke up in the night. Saved a walk to the
kitchen.

"I'd better go see to my chicken. I'll leave you
to unpack," May said.

Robin put her things away. Then she took a
long look at the room. Judge Fox—Ann—had
thought of everything. Or maybe it was May?
Lots of pink writing paper on the writing table.
Postcards of New York City. A radio and a little

clock. Even a book of stamps and some post-card stamps.

After dinner, Robin had a long talk with Judge Fox. She told her about her mother. What she looked like, and all her doings. And about Daddy and their home. But talking to her was not quite as much fun as talking to Mr. Hill. Somehow she didn't feel like talking to her about Ricky-Micky. She might think it silly.

That night, Robin went to bed early. She fell into a deep sleep. When she woke, she couldn't think where she was. She looked at the time. Ten after ten—wow!

There was a tap at the door and May came in. "Good morning, Robin." She went to the window. "How about I let some sunshine in? We've got a fine day coming up."

"I slept like a log," Robin said, stretching. "Look how late it is! I guess Judge Fox has had her breakfast by now."

"You'd better believe it," May said. "Had it and gone. The Judge is one busy woman. I'm afraid you won't see much of each other, not during the day." As Robin started to get out of bed, May put out a hand. "You stay right there and I'll bring you some breakfast."

"Breakfast in *bed*! I only get that at home when I'm sick—*really* sick," Robin said. "I don't even eat breakfast some days. I'm getting too fat."

"That you're not," May said. "You're put together just right. I don't hold with skinny young girls." At the door she turned, taking something out of her pocket. "The Judge told me to give you this—it's a street map."

The map had a note on it. "You might like to walk over to Fifth Avenue and get the bus downtown. You'll see quite a lot."

Go for a bus ride alone, Robin thought. She wasn't used to going places all by herself. At home there was always Bunny or Buzz or some other kid to go places with her.

She began to smile, thinking. She knew what she would do. When May came back with breakfast—oranges, two eggs, and little hot rolls—Robin said, "It would be fun to have someone to go with on the bus. Judge Fox told Mother there was a Ricky living across the hall. Or maybe it was Micky—Mother couldn't quite hear."

27

"It's Ricky," May said. "But I don't know. I'm not sure Miss Field lets him go on the bus."

Robin stared at her. Why ever not? What kind of boy was Ricky? She couldn't have heard right—or perhaps May was kidding her?

"I've got to get to work now," May said. "When you're through—and mind you eat it all— I'll take you across the hall to Miss Field. Right?"

"Right." Robin smiled. She was sure, now, that May had been kidding. I'll wear the city-print shirt, she thought.

When Robin was dressed, May looked at her from head to toe. "You sure look pretty," she said. "And Ricky sure likes pretty girls." She took Robin across the hall and rang the bell of Number 3. "Miss Field should be in. She doesn't often go out in the mornings."

The door opened and a sweet-faced little woman smiled at them. "Good morning, Miss Field," May said. "This is Robin Green. She's staying with the Judge."

"So I heard." Miss Field shook hands with Robin. "Do come in, dear."

"I'll leave her with you. I've got my work to do,"

May said. "Robin wants to meet your Ricky, she told me."

"Then she shall, right away." Miss Field sounded pleased. "I think he's out on the fire escape. Come on through the kitchen, Robin, and I'll call him." In the kitchen, she took a handful of peanuts from a dish on the table. "He'll come fast when he sees these."

There was a noise at the window. As Robin stared, a little monkey jumped into the room. He came up to Robin and sat in front of her, looking up into her face.

"These little monkeys make wonderful pets," Miss Field said. "Ricky is just as good and sweet as he can be."

5

Robin kept staring, wide-eyed. This wasn't—oh, it *couldn't be*—

"Shake hands with Robin, Ricky," Miss Field said. And to Robin, "Here, give him a peanut, dear, or he may jump at you for it."

Ricky was a *monkey*. Robin began to laugh. She couldn't help it. After all those silly dreams about Ricky taking her out to dinner. With music and dancing and pink lights. She bit her lip but she could not stop shaking with laughter.

Miss Field looked at her coldly. "Why, Robin, whatever's the matter with you? You must have seen a monkey before. *Do* stop laughing. You'll hurt his feelings!"

But the little monkey did not look hurt. He was quite happy, taking the shell off his peanut.

Robin tried to pull herself together. "I'm sorry, Miss Field," she said. "But you see, I thought Ricky was a *boy*. I've even been dreaming that he would show me around in the city!"

30

"A *boy*?" Miss Field looked at Ricky as if to make sure he had *not* turned into a boy. "Whatever made you think that?"

"It was something Judge Fox said to Mother. She said I could have fun with Ricky—and Mother and Daddy and I just thought Ricky was a boy."

It was Miss Field's turn to laugh. "I see," she said. She looked from Robin to Ricky as he put out his paw for another peanut. "I'm afraid Ricky can't take you out to dinner. But you can have a little fun with him any time you like. He loves to be taken for walks."

"How long have you had him?" Robin wanted to know. She was watching how nicely Ricky shelled his peanuts. He really was a dear little monkey. Of course she had seen monkeys before, but only in the zoo. It might be fun to get to know one close up.

"I got him four years ago. I saw him in a pet shop one day. He was all alone in the big window—and he just *looked* at me!" Miss Field reached to pat Ricky's head. "I just marched right in and bought him." She laughed. "You should have seen the doorman's face when I walked into the building! They're used to cats and dogs, but hardly monkeys.''

Robin touched Ricky's soft fur. "He's very tame, isn't he?''

"Oh, yes. This kind of monkey is noted for being good with people. Ricky's quite at home in the apartment—he acts like a little boy. He can make his own fun but he loves having someone to play with.''

She brought the monkey's leash. "I let him run loose inside but I always tie him up when he's on the fire escape. If I didn't, he would run up onto the roof, and then he might get lost.'' She went pale at the very thought.

Robin watched as Miss Field let Ricky climb out through the kitchen window. She fastened the leash carefully to the railing. "You might like to play with him for a few minutes, Robin,'' she said.

Robin took a peanut from the dish, hid it in one hand, and held both hands out to Ricky. When he picked the hand with the nut in it, he jumped up and down. But he did not eat it. He gave it

back to Robin, and the game started again.

Suddenly he curled up in a corner of the fire escape and went to sleep. Robin looked at him, thinking how funny he was. He had quite a set-up out there. A red mat, some plants, a bowl of water, some toys. Even a little chair.

While Ricky slept, Robin took a look around. There was not much to see. A few yards, all empty. And the yards and backs of the houses on the next street.

One house surprised her. It was an old brown-stone. At first look, it seemed small. But maybe it only looked small because of the high, new-looking apartment buildings on each side of it. Robin counted its windows. Yes, it was quite big. If it stood alone, you would see how large it really was.

It had a dark, closed-up look. All the windows were shut, and so was the back door. The yard had once been a garden. Robin could see a paved part, with big stone jars that had held flowering plants. Two tall old trees hung over the garden, and a fence cut it off from the yards around it. The house looked as if no one was living there, as if it had been shut up for a long time.

When Robin was leaving, Miss Field said, "Would you like to take Ricky for a walk some time? It's really fun—that is, if you like meeting people. Everyone stops to talk to Ricky and ask all about him."

"I'd love to take him," Robin said. "Maybe tomorrow."

That afternoon she walked over to Fifth Avenue and took the bus downtown. As they rolled along, the woman next to her, guessing that Robin was new to the city, pointed things out. Central Park. The Metropolitan Museum of Art. The Hotel Plaza with its fountain. I'll skip the museum, Robin thought. But there was a zoo in the park, wasn't there? And maybe she could go to one of the open-air shows.

That evening, at dinner, Judge Fox laughed as Robin told her she had thought Ricky was a boy. "I *did* say he was a monkey," she said. "But there was so much noise on the line. Anyway, how do you like him?"

Robin smiled. "Oh, he's really something. I'm

35

going to take him for a walk tomorrow."

"It's too bad we've nothing but a little monkey to keep you company," Judge Fox said. "But in summer so many of the young people I know are out of town. However, the Baker girls—Peg and Merry—are coming to lunch on Sunday with their mother. If you like them, you can go to some of the shows together."

"Oh, please don't worry about me," Robin said. "I've made all kinds of plans. I'm going to do some window shopping in the morning—and I think I'll get a bicycle for an hour and take a ride in the park." She wondered if Ricky would ride a bike with her. They'd have everyone staring!

When she went to bed, Judge Fox asked her if her room was all right. "Some of my guests are afraid because the room is next to the kitchen— with the fire escape. But there's a good lock on the window, and of course they'd have to move the screen."

Robin laughed. "I might be afraid of a tiger, but not much else!"

Before getting into bed, Robin went to the kitchen for one of May's cookies. She thought of the closed-up brownstone house and stood for a minute, looking at it across the yard. She wondered again why it was closed up. It looked as if no one had lived there for a long time. Maybe years.

As she was turning away, she thought she saw a low light in one of the upper rooms. She stared, startled. Then the light went out, but it showed again in another room. Like a turned-down oil lamp, or a candle.

Most likely a reflection, Robin thought sleepily. She could not keep her eyes open. She was much too tired for guessing games about lights. Tomorrow she would ask Judge Fox to tell her about the closed-up house. Getting into bed, she fell asleep almost at once.

6

Robin woke up early the next day. Breakfast in bed was fine but she felt she should get up and have it with Judge Fox. And Judge Fox seemed pleased to have someone to talk with as she ate.

When Robin asked about the closed-up house, Judge Fox looked surprised. "You don't miss much, do you?" she said. "I've had many friends sleeping in your room but no one has ever asked me about that house."

"Maybe they didn't look out the window," Robin said. "I saw it when I was sitting playing with Ricky. The house looked small with those high buildings on each side of it, but I guess it's really quite big."

"It is. A fine old brownstone, built about a hundred years ago. The Stone family built it, and Stones have always lived in it. It was a happy house until a few years ago, full of people and lights and music. And then—" She stopped, remembering. "I don't know if I should tell you. It's not a pretty story."

"Oh, do, please!" Robin said. "You can't stop now."

"It's a murder story—with more than one murder, though the second one was perhaps more like an accident," Judge Fox said. "The Stone family was closer than many families, and the children seemed in no hurry to leave home. April, the girl, was a fine pianist. She played often in the city and was beginning to be known in other countries, too. Jon, the son, was making a name for himself as a painter." She was quiet for a minute. "April and her brother were both killed, and their mother nearly went out of her mind with sorrow."

"How—how did it happen?"

"Someone broke into the house. Whoever he was, he most likely came to steal, because the place was full of fine old silver and china. April must have waked when he went into her room. The police think that she cried out and he held a pillow over her face to quiet her. But Jon heard something, and came running. From what the police say, there was a fight. Jon was pushed through a window and fell to the street. He died almost at once.''

"But what about the others in the house?" Robin asked. "The father and mother—and the help. Didn't anyone else hear?"

Judge Fox shook her head. "The house was shut up for the summer and the help were at the Stones' place on Long Island. April and Jon had come to the city to meet a friend who was returning from France in a ship that docked early in the morning. They had talked about staying in a hotel, but they decided it would be fun to sleep in their own home.''

"Fun!" Robin said. "Oh, the poor things!"

"It was hardest on Mrs. Stone. Mr. Stone took her away, to Italy, I believe. They never came back here. I don't know why they didn't get rid of the house. Perhaps because it had been in their family for so long and they hated the thought of its being made into apartments or anything like that.''

"Maybe they'll remember the happy times they

had in it, and come back some day,'' Robin said thoughtfully.

"Let's hope so. It's a sad place to have in the block."

After hearing the story, Robin found it hard to keep her mind off the Stone family. So, when Judge Fox left for court, she went across to Miss Field's and asked if she might take Ricky out. It would be nicer than thinking about that terrible story.

"Ricky would love a walk!" Miss Field said. "Just be careful to keep him on the leash—and better not go farther than around the block." She smiled. "Even that will take you quite a time. Ricky stops to look at everything from puppies to bits of paper."

"Walking a monkey will be really weird," Robin said. "I know a girl back home who doesn't like dogs. But she always takes the next-door dog for a run because she thinks she might bump into some nice, dog-loving boy!"

The little monkey was jumping up and down in the hall. When Miss Field put the leash on him, he seemed to know that Robin was going to take him out, and he pulled her along to the door. But once there, he stopped, looking up at Miss Field.

"Is he afraid to go with me?" Robin asked.

"Oh no, it's not that. He's never afraid of anyone. It's his *cap*," Miss Field said. "He never goes out without it." She opened a drawer in the kitchen and brought back a little red cap. "Here, Ricky!"

Ricky pulled the cap over one ear, and Robin laughed. "What the well-dressed monkey will wear," she said. "Come on, Ricky. Let's go!"

She felt like a movie star as they walked down the street. This was really something to write home about. Maybe she could draw a picture of Ricky to send to Bunny or Buzz. Though he *was* a bit of a clown, Buzz loved animals of all kinds.

It happened just as Miss Field had said. Everyone on the block stopped to talk to Ricky. Most of them asked where Miss Field was. "I'm surprised she lets you take Ricky out without her," one woman said. "She's so careful about that little animal."

Robin was glad of the leash when Ricky suddenly jumped at an old man's pocket. "Down, Ricky," she cried. *"Down."*

"Don't blame Ricky, blame me," the old man said. "I always have candy in my pocket, and Ricky gets a bit. But today my grandchild has cleaned me out. Too bad, Ricky."

It took some time to get the monkey to move along. But he moved faster when they rounded the corner. A lady came out of Kit's Cake Shop, carrying a white box. "Why, Ricky, pet!" she called. "Come here!" She opened the box and took out a pink cake. "He loves this kind," she told Robin. "Won't you have one, too?"

"No, thank you. I had a big breakfast," Robin said. New Yorkers were always eating in the street, she thought—and what a mess they made! Dropping candy wrappers and tossing peanut shells on the sidewalk, and everything. People were much more careful in the Middle West.

When they turned into the next street, Robin remembered that the Stone house was in the middle of the block. She would be able to see what it looked like from the front.

As she neared the house, a boy from Sam's Dry Cleaner's stopped his bike beside her. "Hi," he said. "Does Ricky want a ride today? Miss Field lets him, so long as I keep hold of his leash."

Robin thought a minute. "Better not today, thank you," she said. "It's the first time I've taken him out, so I think I'll hang onto him." She added, "I wanted to take a look at the Stone house. I've just heard the story and I keep thinking about it."

The boy nodded. "Kind of throws you, don't it? A real murder story. They never found who did it and the people never came back here to live."

Together they looked up at the dark windows, the steps littered with bits of paper, the two stone urns that once held plants. "Gives you the creeps, don't it?" the boy said. He moved closer to Robin. "Do you think there's *ghosts* in there?"

"Of course not! There's no such thing as ghosts!"

"That's what *you* think!" The boy looked at the

44

house again. "Don't be too sure! If there's no ghosts, how come I saw a white face peeping out from the top window?"

Robin stared at him. "You saw a *face*?"

"Last week, it was. It was there a minute, and then—then it was gone. But I sure did see it. A girl's face. White and thin—and scary."

Robin tried to laugh. What sort of secret was the brownstone hiding? "You dreamed it!" she said. "What time of day was it?"

"Around ten, and dark. I went to a movie after work, and I was just heading for the bus to go home."

Suddenly Robin remembered the light she had seen. It looked as if there *was* someone in the house. She wondered if she should tell this boy about the light.

But, at that moment, he jumped onto his bike and, with a wave of his hand, went on his way.

7

Robin did some shopping the next day. A pipe for her father. An art book for her mother. That night, Judge Fox took her to see a show at Radio City Music Hall. As they were leaving, she told Robin, "I used to love walking in the streets of New York late at night. But you can't do that now—it isn't safe any more."

It was after midnight when Robin went to bed. She looked out of the window at the brownstone house for a time, but there were no lights. I must have seen a reflection, she thought.

Then, as she was turning away, she saw not one but two dim lights in the basement. Her heart beat faster. There's something there, she thought. But it's not a ghost. Ghosts don't need lights!

She was almost asleep when the thought came to her. Why don't I go over and peep through the basement window? I might be able to see who is in the house.

It would be easy enough to go down the fire escape, cross the yard, and climb over the low wall. She might even jump it—she had won the high jump last year at school.

But what if someone saw her? Someone from one of the apartments who happened to be looking out of a window?

It wouldn't be likely, Robin thought. There was nothing to see, and no one ever seemed to look out. And if somebody *did* see, and called down to her, she could say she had dropped something from the fire escape and was looking for it.

Tomorrow night would be a good time. Judge Fox was going out. "It's a dinner I have to go to, and I'll be home very late," she told Robin. "Would you like me to get Jane Winter to go to a movie with you?" Jane worked in her office.

"Oh, no thanks," Robin had said. "I don't at all mind being by myself. It's time I started some letters—and I want to draw a picture of Ricky. I might do that."

The next morning she took herself to the

Statue of Liberty. She met some nice kids on the boat going over and they had fun cheering each other on, up the 128 steps of the winding stairway and into Miss Liberty's head.

In the afternoon she washed her hair with something called Flower Fresh. But her hair smelled like cabbage, so she washed it again with some stuff she found in the bathroom.

When her hair was dry, Robin went to Miss Field's to start on her drawing of Ricky. She would have to make two, because Miss Field had asked for one. "I have a snap that a friend took," she said, "but it would be much nicer to have a drawing, signed by *you*. I can get it framed and hang it on my bedroom wall."

Ricky was jumpy at first. Robin made him wear his red cap, so he thought he must be going for a walk. But Miss Field got him to sit quietly. She fed him peanuts and it took him time to take off the shells.

With her rough drawings finished, Robin went back to the apartment. When the bell rang at three o'clock, she told May, "I'll get it." To her surprise, it was the boy she had talked with in front of the brownstone house. "Well, hi," he said. "I didn't know Judge Fox had any kids!"

Kids! Robin gave him a cold look. "She hasn't. And if you're talking about *me*, I'm no kid. My mother is an old friend of Judge Fox and I'm staying here while my parents are in France."

"Okay, okay," the boy said. He handed Robin a blue suit on a hanger. "She's a nice lady, the Judge." He looked past Robin to where May was coming out of the living room. "Hi, there, Mrs. Childs."

"Hi, Tom," May said. "I suppose you feel like one of my cookies?"

"I feel like two, or maybe three," Tom said, smiling. "I'll have to eat 'em on my rounds, though. Very busy today."

While May was in the kitchen, Robin quickly told Tom about the lights she had seen in the brownstone house. He whistled. "Wow! Who do you think it is? Can't be the folks back. They'd not creep around with low lights. It's gotta be ghosts, like I said!"

"Ghosts don't need lights," Robin said. She lowered her voice. "I'm going to try to find out

49

who's there. I can cross our yard into theirs and maybe see something through their basement windows.''

'Wow,'' Tom said again. "You better take care!''

"Want to come along?'' Robin asked, to see what he would say.

"Not me, sister.'' He backed away. "I don't go for spirits!'' He took the cookies which May brought and put them into his pocket. "Thanks a lot, Mrs. Childs.'' And to Robin, "You watch your step!''

After supper, Robin put the finishing touches to her drawings of Ricky. They were really life-like. She smiled, thinking how pleased Miss Field would be. She was so fond of that little monkey.

When May had left for home, Robin looked at the time. Nine-thirty, and already night. She put on her dark slacks and shirt. That way she would not be so easy to see.

She went through the kitchen without turning on the light and climbed out onto the fire escape. No light shone from the apartment below. The people were out or in their front rooms. Moving

50

quickly, she made her way down the fire escape and jumped lightly to the ground.

Safe in the yard, she looked back at the building she had just left. Miss Field's kitchen window was closed, with Ricky safely inside. There were a few lights shining from other windows, but no one was looking out.

The night was dark, with no moon, but there was enough light to see her way. At the end of the yard, Robin came to the wall which bordered the garden of the brownstone house. It was not very high and there were good footholds. She climbed up easily, and jumped down on the other side.

She made her way under one of the tall old trees, past two white benches and a little fence which must once have been pretty with climbing roses. Maybe the young man, Bob, used to set up his easel here, Robin thought. And paint the old trees, or the sky, or an airplane overhead. Perhaps the family gave dances—the house was big enough to have a ballroom—and the dancers would come out to rest on the benches.

Moving very quietly, she went up to one of the

windows. Peering through the pane, she saw a light gleaming, and drew back quickly. Not a ghost, Robin thought. This was someone human. Someone moving about with a lamp or a candle.

She moved to the next window and the light moved, too. It must all be one room, she thought, maybe a big kitchen.

Then she came to the back door. Gently, she tried the knob. To her surprise, the door was not locked. The knob turned easily, and she pushed the door open a little wider.

She was about to poke her head around the door when she heard a sound. Someone was behind the door. She could hear breathing.

A hand shot out and held her above the elbow. "Don't yell," a voice said. She was pulled inside and the door shut gently. She heard a key turn in the lock. "In here," the voice said. "Where we can see you!"

8

"Don't yell," the voice said again, and Robin found herself being pushed through another doorway into a big kitchen. Her arm began to hurt and she pulled around to see who was holding her.

It was a boy. In the dim light, she could make out his face and his dark hair. It was a good-looking face, with bright eyes and a strong chin. He looked older than she by a year or two.

"Whoever you are, let go of my arm," Robin said. "I'm not afraid, but I'm getting black and blue." She added coldly, "I won't yell."

The boy let her go. "Sorry about that," he said. "I don't go for hurting girls. But don't make any noise. Elly, bring the candle over here."

"It's pretty near out." A girl came from the back of the room, holding a candle in her hand. She was small and thin. Much younger than I am, Robin thought.

"I'll put the lamp on," the boy said. "No one will see us if we keep the light away from the

54

windows." He went off into the darkness, calling back, "You two go sit at the table."

The girl went before Robin across the room and pulled out a chair at the big kitchen table. "Here," she said. *"Oh—"* The candle went out, and they heard the boy laugh. "Elly's scared of the dark," he said, but kindly. He went over to the table and set down a small oil lamp. Then he took a chair himself and sat down, staring at Robin.

In the lamplight, she could see him more clearly. A *good* face, she thought. Clever, too. A boy you could like.

"Now, give," he said. "Where do you come from and why are you peeping into windows in the night?"

"I'm staying in a house just back of this one. I don't live there. It's Judge Fox's apartment. I've seen some lights in this house off and on —" She stopped. The boy had started nervously. "Do you mean a real judge?" he asked sharply. "Or is it a name—like Cap or Doc?"

Robin laughed. "Oh, Judge Fox is real enough. She's a judge in the Children's Court."

The girl Elly gave a little cry. "Oh, Len—we'd better move on!"

"Judge Fox hasn't seen the lights, and I haven't said anything about them," Robin said. "I don't think anyone has noticed them but me. People don't look out of their back windows—there's really nothing to look at." She remembered Ricky, and smiled. "Unless you count Ricky, and he's only a little monkey."

"We've seen him out on the fire escape," the boy said. "He's there every day." He laughed shortly. "I had trouble stopping Elly from going over to pet him."

"Does he belong to Judge Fox?" Elly asked.

"Oh, no, that's not our apartment. Ricky is Miss Field's pet. She lives in the apartment across from ours."

"I see her on the street sometimes, with the monkey," Elly said. "She likes him a lot, doesn't she? Isn't she scared to leave him out on the fire escape?"

"Oh, he's safe there. He's on a leash, tied to the rail," Robin told her. "Anyway, I don't suppose anyone would want to steal a little monkey."

"You never know," the boy said. He changed

56

the subject. "Let's hear more about *you*. How come you came over here?"

Robin smiled at him. "I'm nosy, I guess. Now, you tell me about yourselves. I've told you who I am and how I came to be here. But I don't know where you two came from—I don't even know your names."

"I'm Elly White and he's Len Pond," the girl began.

"And you don't need to know where we've come from," Len said quickly. "I'll tell you this much. We're runaways. We met on a bus and I—well, I could see that Elly had to have someone around to look after her."

"We both wanted to see New York," Elly said. Her face darkened. "But it hasn't been much fun."

Maybe Len was pleased by Robin's interest, because he took up the story. "We were sleeping in the park, but Elly caught a cold and it hung on. So I thought I'd better find a roof. We saw this house one day but there was no way to get in." He frowned, remembering. "Then one morning we saw a man go up the steps—checking some-

57

thing, I guess. Anyway, he left the door open a bit, so Elly and I ran inside and hid till he left."

"And no one's been here again," Elly said. "It's been real nice. Beds and everything." She smiled. "I'm sleeping in a big pink room, and Len likes the couch downstairs."

"But the water's turned off, and the gas and lights." Len made a face. "We have to bring water from the park. I got a camp stove from a store, so we can boil water and heat stuff to eat."

"What do you do for money?" Robin wanted to know. I could give them some, she thought. I won't need *all* those checks Daddy gave me.

"Oh, Elly has some, but not much," Len said. "And I make a buck off and on. At the bike stand in the park. And helping give donkey rides to little kids."

"I could easily bring you some food," Robin said. They looked as if they could use it. Elly was so thin and pale. And Len wasn't much fatter, though he looked strong enough.

Elly was pleased, but Len shook his head. "Forget it," he said. "We're doing okay. Elly likes it here, but we'll be on our way pretty soon, before our luck gives out."

"But I'd like to see you again, and help if I can," Robin said. I want to know more about you, she thought. A lot more. Why you left home. What you plan to do when winter comes.

"I could use a change of clothes," Elly said hopefully. "There's dresses and things here, in the bedroom. But I don't want to take anything, and Len doesn't want me to." She looked at Len. "Couldn't Robin come just once more? We could leave the basement door unlocked in the front of the house."

"It's bad enough that she's come once," Len said. He put his hand on Robin's arm, pushing her gently toward the back door. There he said, "Want me to give you a leg up over the fence?"

"Oh, no, thanks. I made it over, and I'll make it back."

"Good-bye, then," Len said. "Forget you ever saw us. You said you wanted to help us, and that's the best way you can."

He watched Robin step into the yard. Then, very quietly, he closed the door, and she heard the key turn in the lock.

It was darker now, but a few lights showed from apartment windows. Going back was as easy as coming over—until Robin reached the fire escape. Then she stopped, startled. The ladder was much higher from the ground than she had thought. This was not going to be easy.

Backing away, she gave a running jump and her hands touched the bottom rung. But even if she could cling to the rung, she would not be able to pull herself up. I'm too heavy, she thought. I'd have to have someone to help me.

If Len were here, she could have made it by standing on his shoulders. But Len was back in the brownstone house, behind a locked door.

And, if she went back and tapped, she was sure that he wouldn't open it.

9

Now how do I get in, Robin wondered. She tried the basement door, but it was locked. She tapped sharply. Then, putting her ear to the door, she heard steps coming. The door opened a crack and an elderly man looked at her.

"I'm so sorry to bother you," Robin said, "but will you please let me in? I'm staying in Judge Fox's apartment." As he made no move, she went on, "I was looking for something—in the back of the yard." It was almost true.

The door opened wider. "Well, you don't look very dangerous," the man said, "so come on in. But may I ask how you got into the yard?"

Robin laughed. "By the fire escape—but I didn't think about how I'd get back. And that ladder's just too high!"

"And a good thing, too!" He led her out to the stairs. "Up you go, then. And next time you drop something, just ask me and I'll get it for you."

Back in the apartment, Robin locked the

kitchen window. In her room, she undressed quickly and got into bed. She lay awake for a long time, thinking. She meant to see those kids again, no matter what Len said. She would bring Elly something to wear.

Then she remembered that back door. It had been open when she went over, but only because Len was waiting behind it to pull her inside. He had locked it after her just now, and it would stay that way. Elly might like to see her, but Len had no wish to meet with Robin Green ever again.

In the next few days, Robin was busy. There was the tea with the Baker girls. Nice enough girls, but a little old for her. On her own, she took the bus to Chinatown and Wall Street, joining the other out-of-towners as they walked around. And of course she went up to the top of the World Trade Center to look down on the city.

Judge Fox took time off to go with her to the World Trade Center but Robin did not really see much of her the rest of the time. She was busy in court, and was glad that Robin could get along so well without her.

Robin did not forget the runaways in the brownstone house. She wondered how they were doing for food and wished she could get a change of clothes to poor Elly.

She thought of going over there one night and leaving some things outside the back door. But they might never open that door. Or someone in one of the apartments might see the things and wonder. Maybe it was better to give up the idea.

On Friday night, when she and Judge Fox were coming back from an evening at the Bakers', they were startled to see police officers at Miss Field's door. Judge Fox spoke to them quickly. "Has anything happened to Miss Field, Officer?"

"We don't know yet, ma'am," one of them said. "She called the station."

The door opened and Miss Field looked out. She was pale and shaking. "Oh, I'm so glad you came so quickly," she said. "Judge Fox— Robin—Ricky's gone!"

"Your son, ma'am?" The two officers looked at her.

"Ricky is Miss Field's pet monkey," Judge Fox

told them quietly. Steps sounded on the stairs. "Maybe we'd better talk inside?"

"Oh, yes—yes." In the living room, Miss Field turned to the officers. "Ricky was out on the fire escape, tied and quite safe, I thought. He didn't want to come in yet. He loves it out there when it is dark." Tears came to her eyes. "I wish I'd brought him in!"

"May we see where he was when you left him, ma'am?"

"Of course you may!" Miss Field led the officers into the kitchen, and Judge Fox and Robin followed. "There!" she said. "And now he's gone, leash and all!"

"Could he have got the leash undone?" one of the men asked.

"Ricky? Oh, no. Of course he's very clever with his paws but *I'm* very good at knots. I was a Girl Scout when I was young."

"If he got loose, he'll have gone up to the roof. Or down into the yard," the older man said. "Joe, you try the roof. I'll take a look around the yard."

"That will take a little time," Judge Fox said, as the men climbed out onto the fire escape. "Come and sit down, Miss Field—I'll make you a cup of tea."

"Let me," Robin said. She wanted to help. Poor Miss Field, she thought. I don't know what she'll do if they don't find Ricky.

When the men came back, Miss Field jumped up eagerly. "No luck yet, ma'am," the younger one said kindly. "But he's sure to show up somewhere. Do the people around here know him?"

"Oh, yes," Miss Field said. A little color came back into her face. "Ricky has lots of friends, all around the block—and on the avenues, too."

"Well, ma'am, there's not much you can do till morning," the older officer said. "Then you can call the A.S.P.C.A. first thing. Someone may have turned him in by then. And call everyone you know on the block."

"He may come back in the night," Miss Field said hopefully. "I'll leave the window open for him."

65

"No, ma'am, better not do that," the older officer said. "If he comes back, he'll wait. You can look out from time to time."

"Yes, of course. I won't sleep a wink. I'll sit up in a chair."

"That wouldn't be very wise," Judge Fox said. "Why not do as the officer says? Go to bed now, and in the morning we'll call the A.S.P.C.A."

"Let me stay with you," Robin said. "I can stay awake while you take a nap, and then I'll take one while you watch for Ricky." She turned to Judge Fox. "That will be okay, won't it?"

Judge Fox nodded at her. "You can make up your sleep tomorrow. Go and get what you need for the night. I'll stay with Miss Field till you get back."

This at least took Miss Field's mind off Ricky for a time. When Robin got back, she found the sofa in the living room made up for her to sleep on. There was a glass of milk and a plate of cookies on the coffee table.

"I'll say good night now," Judge Fox said. "I have to be in court early tomorrow." At the door, she turned. "And, oh, Robin—I'll be very late coming home tomorrow night. I have to go out to Long Island to see an old friend whose son is in some sort of trouble. I'll call you at home at eight or nine tomorrow night—and if there's no answer I'll call you here."

Miss Field, worn out, fell asleep quickly and slept heavily.

There was not much sleep for Robin that night. At every sound, she crept out into the kitchen to see if Ricky had come home.

But there was nothing on the fire escape, no sign of the little monkey. By five o'clock, there was enough daylight to see down into the yards. But Ricky was not there.

10

By seven, Miss Field was wide awake. Hearing her push up the kitchen window, Robin hurried out. Miss Field was just about to climb out on the fire escape.

"Come back—let me do that!" Robin cried. She caught the old lady by the arm. "You make us some coffee while I take a look out."

"I don't see him," Miss Field said, looking down into the yard. "He's not down there. Oh, Robin, what shall I do? I had such terrible dreams."

"Dreams don't mean anything," Robin told her. "You should hear some of mine." She came back into the kitchen. "Ricky will be okay, you'll see. No one would hurt him, he's so sweet. And Judge Fox will call the A.S.P.C.A. soon now—Ricky may be there already."

She pretended to be hungry to give Miss Field something to do. The old lady made coffee and toast and boiled an egg for Robin. "I can't eat a thing," she said. "Not till Ricky comes home."

At five past nine the bell rang. Judge Fox stood there. "I've called the A.S.P.C.A.," she said. "They're going to send a man over. He'll search the roofs to see if Ricky has got stuck anywhere. They're used to saving birds and cats." She smiled at Miss Field. "But they seem fairly sure that Ricky has gone into someone's apartment. If so, the people will call the A.S.P.C.A. You must just try not to worry."

Half an hour later, the man from the A.S.P.C.A. came. He asked a good many questions about Ricky. How old was he? Was he good tempered? Was he likely to bite? Was he hard to catch?

"Ricky *never* bites," Miss Field said.

"Not anyone he knows," Robin added.

"Well, I'll use a net, ma'am," the man said. "He doesn't know me, and a monkey bite could be nasty." He let himself out of the kitchen window and headed for the roof.

When he came back, he shook his head. "He's not up there, ma'am, that's for sure. So he must be in someone's apartment. Mind if I use your phone to call the office?"

69

Ricky was not at the A.S.P.C.A. "But don't you get upset, ma'am," the man said kindly. "Stay near the phone. You're sure to get a call sooner or later. Not many people would want to keep a monkey. A kitten, maybe, but not a monkey."

After the man had gone, May rang the bell. She put her arms around Miss Field. "Now don't you get upset," she said. "He'll be back. I feel it in my bones."

"Miss Field hasn't eaten a thing," Robin told her. "She ought to have some breakfast. She may be in for a long wait."

"That's what I've come for. To take you over to our place to eat," May said. "Robin can stay here in case anyone calls—and she can keep an eye on the fire escape, too."

When Miss Field came back, she looked a little happier. "May makes me feel better. She's so sure Ricky is safe. She tells me I must have faith —and I *will*." She sat down by the telephone. "I'll call everyone I can think of who may have seen Ricky. And I'll ask the boy from the cleaner's. And that girl—if she comes back today."

"Girl?" Robin said. "What girl, Miss Field?"

"The girl I was talking to at the door—when

70

Ricky got away. She kept me some time. She was looking for work. Errands to run, and such."

"What did she look like?" Robin said. She had a funny feeling inside.

"Oh, small. And very thin. She seemed such a nice young girl."

Small, and very thin. It sounded like Elly. But why would she be looking for work? Len had certainly said they would be moving on soon. And how did she know where Miss Field's apartment was?

Robin made an excuse to leave. She wanted to get away from Miss Field—to *think.*

Back in the apartment, she closed the door of her room behind her and tried to remember what she had said to Len and Elly. Yes, she had told them that Miss Field lived across the hall from Judge Fox! Elly could easily get the apartment number from the mailbox. But *why*? And what was Len doing while Elly was at Miss Field's door?

Robin's mind whirled. Could the runaways have taken Ricky—for *ransom*? They might think Miss Field had money and would be glad to pay to get her pet back.

71

Len was clever enough to think up a plan. He could have sent Elly to Miss Field's to keep the old lady talking. And then—then he could have climbed the fire escape, taken Ricky, and gone back with him to the brownstone house!

That was what must have happened. It was well thought out. Robin felt sick. She had liked Len. He had not struck her as a bad boy. Using the Stones' house wasn't really *very* terrible. They had not done any damage, or stolen anything.

But taking Ricky away when they knew he was an old lady's pet—that was an awful thing to do! If they were caught, they might be put in prison.

Robin frowned. She had to find out for sure. But she couldn't do anything yet. Not till tonight. After May left for home, she would go across the yard, as she had done before, and knock at the back door of the brownstone house.

But what if Len wouldn't open the door?

I'll take a stone with me, Robin thought. I—I'll break a window. That will frighten them. I'll call through the window and tell them I'll get the police if they don't open up!

11

Now that she was sure she knew where Ricky was, Robin could not wait for the day to pass. She spent most of it with Miss Field, trying to help her to be brave. After a time, she ran out of things to say to cheer her up.

"Why don't you take a little nap?" she asked finally. "And I'll go round to the store and get some bananas. Then you'll have something to give Ricky for a treat when he gets home."

First, though, she took a walk around the block and looked at the brownstone house. Everything was dark, closed. She could see no way of getting in. If she rang the bell, Len and Elly would not answer. If she banged on the door, people would wonder why. No, there was no easy way. She would have to get in at the back, as she had planned.

In the store, she bought some bananas. Then she thought of a can of peanuts. She might need them to keep Ricky quiet when she found him.

She was taking down a can when a girl came up to the shelf. A small, very thin girl. "Elly!" Robin cried, dropping the can of nuts in her surprise. "Elly—wait!" But Elly gave Robin one scared look and took to her heels.

Pushing her way past some shoppers, Robin rounded the corner to where the bread was. But there was no Elly. Only a fat lady, looking cross. "How about *that*?" she said loudly. "That girl! She almost knocked me down!"

"Did you see which way she went?" Robin asked. "Did she run out of the store?"

"You better believe it! She must have been stealing things to run that way!" The woman looked Robin up and down. "Do you mean you *know* her?"

"I thought she was someone I knew but it couldn't have been. My friends don't steal," Robin said. She walked out of the store but there was no sign of Elly in the street.

When she got back to the apartment, a young woman opened the door. "I'm Miss Field's niece, Bee," she said, holding out her hand. "You must be Robin."

"That's right." Robin smiled and shook hands.

"I've brought the bananas, but I guess there has been no news of Ricky?"

"Not yet. Not a single call, and he's not at the A.S.P.C.A. Poor Aunt Rose!" She took the bananas from Robin. "I can stay with her until tomorrow morning—she may have heard something by then."

"I'm sure she will," Robin said warmly. "Give her my love. I'll come in for a while after I've had supper, tell her."

Sure, now, that Ricky was safe in the brownstone house, Robin had a good appetite for May's cooking that evening. "Thanks for a wonderful supper, May," she said. "If you keep feeding me like this I'll soon be as big as a house." As May began to clear the table, Robin said, "I'd like to take some of that chocolate cake to Miss Field and her niece."

But even the cake did not cheer poor Miss Field. Robin found it hard not to tell her that she knew—or thought she knew—where Ricky was. She stayed chatting with Miss Field and Bee until it began to get dark. She did not want to take a chance of that nice old man's seeing her through the basement window, and of course

76

she did not mean to return through the basement again. Len would have to let her out at the front basement door of the brownstone house— and she must remember to take her key with her.

Back in the apartment, she filled her pocket with peanuts for Ricky and made her way down the fire escape and through the gardens. Going up to a window, she found she had no chance to peep inside. Len and Elly had pulled down the shades, and not even a gleam of light showed.

Robin went to the back door and tapped gently. There was no answer. She tapped again, more loudly. Still no answer. Pressing her ear to the door, she heard a movement inside. They were there, then.

She tapped again and again. Then, after a good look at the apartments across the yards, she picked up a stone and threw it at the basement window, but not hard enough to break it.

For a minute, all was quiet. Then Robin heard the back door opening. Len stood there, his face pale, his eyes angry. "Why can't you leave us alone?" he asked. "Why don't you keep away, like I asked you?"

Robin pushed past him. "Shut the door," she

said. In the big kitchen, the lamp was lit. Elly was sitting at the table, eating. A poor little meal, just some bread and a bit of cheese.

Elly looked smaller and thinner than ever. And she's afraid, Robin thought. Afraid of *me.* But right then she had no time to think about Elly. "Where's Ricky, Len?" she said loudly. "Where's the little monkey?"

Elly gave a cry. She looked at Len, who tried to laugh. "What monkey?" he said. "What do you think this is—a zoo?"

Robin turned on him. "You know what monkey. You took him. You sent Elly to the apartment house to keep Miss Field busy at the door. Then you grabbed Ricky off the fire escape."

Len looked at Elly. "She's out of her head," he said. He waved a hand around the kitchen. "Do you see any little monkey around here, Elly?"

"You hid him when you heard me at the door," Robin said. "But I'll find him if I have to go into every room in this house!" She started toward the kitchen door—and suddenly she saw something on the floor. Something small and red. "Ricky's cap!" she said, picking it up. "So he's here—I knew it!"

78

12

As Len stared at her, saying nothing, Robin turned to Elly. "I don't know what the law says about stealing a pet animal—but I can ask Judge Fox. If Ricky were a little kid, instead of a monkey, you'd be sent to prison for years!"

Elly gave a cry, and Len looked angrily at Robin. "Stop scaring Elly," he said. "And watch your tongue. *Nobody* stole the monkey!"

"He was in our yard," Elly said quickly. "And when I opened the back door a bit, he ran in."

Robin looked from one to the other. She *wanted* to believe them. Len certainly seemed to be telling the truth, but there was still something wrong with their story.

"But how did he get loose?" she asked. "Tell me that!"

"Broke his leash," Len said shortly. "Here, see for yourself!" He took a leash off the table; the end was broken where the knot had been tied to the fire escape. "It was worn where the lady tied it around the rail."

Robin felt as if a load had lifted from her mind. "I see," she said. "I'm sorry for what I said, Len. But—well, why didn't you take him right back to Miss Field? I told you where she lives."

Len went red. "We should have, I know—and it bothered me. But we—I—"

"No, don't blame Len," Elly said quickly. "It was *my* idea to keep Ricky a little while. Just to see if the lady would offer a reward. And—well, I wanted to play with him."

Len frowned. "We've almost run out of money," he said. "Elly went looking for work yesterday, but I don't think she should work. Not with that cough."

"Is that what you were doing at Miss Field's?" Robin asked Elly. "She told me she was talking to a girl at the door."

Elly nodded. "I went to a lot of apartments, but I didn't have any luck."

"Well, I can easily bring you some food," Robin said. "But right now we've got to get Ricky home. This is making Miss Field ill." She looked at Len. "Get him, will you, Len? I'll go with you to the apartment. I'll say I ran into you on the street and you were trying to find out where Ricky

80

lived." A lie, she thought, and I hate lies. But it was the best she could do without getting Len and Elly into trouble. Somehow she couldn't help liking Len. He was doing his best to take care of Elly. Another boy would have taken off by now. She must have been a real drag.

"Okay, okay," Len said. He smiled for the first time since Robin had come in. "I'll be glad to get him home. We don't have anything he likes to eat, and Elly's been crying over him." He crossed the kitchen and opened the door into a hallway. Ricky ran in, chattering, and jumped into Robin's arms.

Robin held him close. "Everything's fine now, Ricky. We're going home." She began to feed him the peanuts.

"Len gave him bread and cheese," Elly said. "It was all we had. He didn't like it, and he made funny noises."

"I was going to get him bananas as soon as I could," Len said. "He wasn't really unhappy. Elly played with him and made him a bed."

"Well, let's get him home *now*," Robin said. "Miss Field is *so* upset."

"We can slip out by the basement door in the

front of the house," Len said. "Elly, wait here."

They left the house one at a time, when there was no one on the block. Robin held Ricky, who chattered excitedly. He seemed to know that he was going home.

Len said nothing until they reached Miss Field's apartment. Then he told Robin, "You do the talking, will you?"

She nodded, ringing the bell. Miss Field's niece opened the door, and let out a cry. "You've found him! Oh, Aunt Rose, come quick! Ricky's back!"

Miss Field came hurrying out. She stared at Ricky as if she couldn't believe her eyes. Then she took him out of Robin's arms and held him tight. "Ricky, Ricky," she said. "I'd begun to think I'd never see you again!"

"Do come in and tell us where you found him," the niece said.

"No, we won't come in, thanks. Miss Field had better feed Ricky right away. He must be hungry," Robin said. "This boy found him some time ago. He's been trying to find out where Ricky lived."

"Oh, how good of you!" Miss Field beamed at Len. "I don't know how to thank you! I've put an ad in the paper, offering a reward—you must have it, of course!"

Len backed away. "No thanks, ma'am. I don't want anything. I—I'm glad I found him for you—" He stopped. Miss Field was hurrying into the apartment.

She was back in a moment, and pushed something into Len's hand. He stood there, uncertain, as if he couldn't make up his mind what to do.

"Do please come in and see Ricky eating," Miss Field said to Robin. She smiled at Len. "And you too, young man."

"No—no, thanks, ma'am. I've got to be going." Without a word to Robin, Len made for the stairs.

Robin stayed at Miss Field's for a time, and they watched Ricky eating. Then he curled up in his basket, and Robin left. "You'll sleep well tonight, Miss Field," she said. "And so will Ricky!"

That night she lay awake for a long time, thinking. She wished she knew why Len and Elly had run away from their homes. She wished she could do something really helpful for them. It wasn't so bad for Len. He was strong. He'd get along somehow. But Elly couldn't take care of herself.

Lying there, she realized how lucky she herself was. She had parents who loved her, a comfortable home, friends—everything to make her happy.

She wondered whether to tell Judge Fox of Len and Elly. Somehow she thought not. After all, she was a judge. She would be on the side of the law. She'd have to report them to the police. What they had done might not be a crime, exactly, but it was certainly wrong. "Breaking and entering," perhaps? Only they hadn't really broken in. They'd gone in through an open door— would that make a difference to the law?

Robin tossed and turned. There must be some way for her to get help for Len and Elly.

She was just falling asleep when she remembered Mr. Hill, the lawyer she had sat next to on the plane. He had given her his card and told her to get in touch with him if she needed him while in New York City.

At the time, it had been a joke, of course. But it wasn't a joke now. Len and Elly might be in real trouble if they were caught in the brownstone house.

Mr. Hill would know how to deal with them. He would know if they were breaking the law or anything. She decided to call him in the morning as soon as Judge Fox had left.

He would tell her what to do.

13

Next morning, Robin telephoned Mr. Hill at his office. "May I ask who's calling?" a voice said.

"Tell him it's Robin Green—the girl he sat next to on the plane," Robin said.

Soon she heard Mr. Hill's voice. "Good morning, Miss Green—or may I call you Robin?"

"Of course," Robin said. "Mr. Hill, do you remember you gave me your card—in case I ran into trouble with the law?" She hurried on. "Well, I'm not in trouble myself but two—two young people I know may be. I really need some help for them."

"I see," Mr. Hill said. "I suppose you have already talked to Judge Fox?"

"Oh, no. She doesn't know anything about it. And I don't want to worry her. She's terribly busy, and she's so tired when she gets home."

"Just a moment, then." She heard him speak to someone. Then his cheerful voice again. "It seems I have to be on East 70th Street this afternoon. Could you meet me at the corner of 70th and Fifth at two o'clock? I'm afraid that will be too late for lunch, but we can have a soda somewhere, and talk.''

"Oh, yes, thank you," Robin said. "That would be fine.''

She told May she was meeting a friend. "You haven't worn that pretty blue dress yet," May said. "It's just the day for it." So Robin put it on and liked herself in it.

Mr. Hill was waiting for her. "Why, Robin, New York certainly suits you," he said, shaking hands. "There's a little place called Mary Lou's near here. Let's try it.''

In Mary Lou's, he found a quiet table and pulled out a chair. "What shall it be? Soda? Ice cream? Cake?''

"An orange soda would be lovely," Robin said.

As soon as they were served, Mr. Hill gave Robin all his attention. "Now let's have it," he said. "I gather that these young people you know have got themselves into trouble?''

Robin frowned. "That's what I want you to tell

me. I'm not really sure, but I think they're breaking the law."

"In what way? Dope? Stealing?"

"Oh, no, nothing like that, I'm sure. I'd better start at the beginning. Do you know the Stone house on East 89th Street?—I mean, do you know what happened there?"

Mr. Hill nodded. "A double murder. Terrible thing. The newspapers were full of it at the time. I think the house is still shut up."

"That's right," Robin said. "Well, the back of Judge Fox's house is right across from the back of the Stone house." She began to tell him all that had happened, and he listened, rubbing his chin slowly.

"Is that what the law would call 'breaking and entering'? " Robin asked.

"But they didn't exactly break in, you say? Have they taken anything from the house, do you know? Stolen something to sell, perhaps?"

"Oh, no, I don't think so. Elly had a little money, and Len picks up a job now and then."

"Well, the Stones aren't here to bring charges. And they may never know about it." He looked at Robin, frowning. "You have no idea where these young people came from, or why they ran away?"

Robin shook her head. "I think Elly would have told me, but Len wouldn't let her."

Mr. Hill finished his coffee. "Seems to me what we have to do is get those kids back where they belong before they run into real trouble. We'll start by getting them out of that house. We might talk them into using the Hot Line."

"What's that?"

"It's a telephone line for runaways. They can call home free and at least put their parents' minds at rest." He was silent for a minute. "I'll tell you what, Robin. You'd better talk to these kids as soon as you can. Then, tomorrow, bring them to my office about three and I'll try to straighten them out."

Robin frowned. "I don't think Len will come. And if *he* won't, Elly won't."

"Well, try and get them there. We'll have to hurry them out of that house and find them somewhere to stay. The Stones' lawyer told me some time ago that they're thinking of coming back to the house."

"*Wow*," Robin said. "Then we'll have to act

89

fast." She looked at her watch. "I mustn't keep you any longer, Mr. Hill. You've been very kind! I'll do my best to get Len and Elly to your office."

When they shook hands, Mr. Hill looked at Robin, smiling. "Do you know something, Robin? You're quite a girl. I wonder how many young people would spend a New York vacation worrying about a pair of runaways."

"It's been exciting, and fun, in a way," Robin said honestly. "I've been doing other things, too. Shows and shopping."

"But nothing as exciting as crashing the Stone house!"

Robin laughed. "No, nothing as exciting as that."

14

There was nothing Robin could do about the runaways that night. Judge Fox took her and the Baker girls to a play. By the time they got home, Robin was ready for bed.

She decided to go to the brownstone house the next morning. Not across the yard, though. In the daytime someone would be sure to see her. She would try tapping softly at the basement door, where Len and she had slipped out with Ricky. Len would guess who it was.

When she got up next morning, she wondered what time to go. When were they likely to get up? About ten? She would wait until then.

She was writing a long letter to Bunny when May came to her room. She held out a note. "Somebody left this in the box. It's for you, Robin."

Robin opened the note. There were just a few lines. "Elly and I are moving on. We left the house okay. Elly cleaned what we used. Thanks

91

for not giving us away to the old lady or anyone. Len."

Moving on. Robin had a sinking feeling. But where would they go? Back to sleep in the park? The nights had been rainy—and Elly still had that cough.

It was too bad, with Mr. Hill ready to help them. Now she would not be likely to see them again. New York City would swallow them up. She could try the park, of course, but it was so large that it would take days to look all over it.

Come to think of it, they just might stay close to 89th Street. They knew the neighborhood and the stores in it.

Robin looked at her watch. It was after ten. She'd better call Mr. Hill and tell him what had happened. She would call from outside, though, where May could not hear. And then—well, she would take Ricky for a walk in the park. She just might come across Len and Elly.

Mr. Hill answered the telephone himself. "Oh, Robin, good," he said. "I see you didn't waste any time. How did it go—are the kids coming to see me?"

"I wish I could say 'yes,' but I can't! They've *gone.* Len left a note for me at our door. It doesn't say anything except that they're moving on. They must have gotten scared."

"That's too bad," Mr. Hill said. "But it's just as well they're out of the house. It's true that the Stones are coming back—they may get there any day. It was in the *Park Avenue News.*

"I'm really worried about Elly—in case they're sleeping in the park," Robin said. "I thought of taking Ricky for a walk and keeping an eye out for them."

"Not a bad idea. There's nothing we can do until we find them. I could call the police—"

"No, don't do that!" Robin said quickly. "Let me try to find them first."

After saying goodbye, she called for Ricky. They walked to Central Park and took a look along some of the paths near Fifth Avenue. Robin even asked a few people who were sitting on benches, but no one had seen a pair who looked at all like Len and Elly.

One lady was frightening. "You seem upset about your friends, dear—and no wonder. The

93

things that happen in the park! Not so much in the daytime, with plenty of people around—but when it's dark!''

Robin felt sick. If Len and Elly started to sleep in the park again, they might be beaten up—*anything*.

Robin went places with the Baker girls in the next few days. But she found it hard to keep her mind off Len and Elly. It worried her that she might never see them again, never know what happened to them. Everywhere she went, she kept looking for them.

On Friday she walked as far as 59th Street, window-shopping. She was just starting for home when she spotted Len in the crowd ahead of her. What luck! Her heart began to beat faster. "Len!" she called. "Len, *wait*!''

He turned, saw her, and raised a hand. Then he came slowly back. "Hi, Robin," he said dully. "I'm in trouble. *Big* trouble this time.''

"What is it? And where's Elly?''

"That's it. That's the trouble. I don't know where she is. I don't even know where to look.''

Robin stared. "But she's always with you!''

94

"She was only supposed to go for a few minutes." They walked along, slowly. "We've been sleeping in the subway. At least it's dry. I wanted to get Elly a room at the Y with some of the money the old lady gave me. But Elly wouldn't stay there." He looked worriedly at Robin. "I should have made her. She's been sort of sick."

"When did you see her last?"

"Two nights ago. At the far end of the park, at 110th Street. We got talking with some kids and they turned out to be sort of wild. They said they were going to break into a store, and they wanted Elly and me to be lookouts—"

"But you didn't—you *wouldn't*—"

Len shook his head. "Elly and I aren't like that. I was trying to think how we could get away without making those kids mad at us. Then Elly said she had a headache and felt funny. So she went across the street to get something from the drugstore." He looked at Robin unhappily. "And she just never came back."

"Did you ask at the drugstore?"

"Oh, sure, but the man said no girl like that had been in. The other kids went off, and I hung

95

around, waiting for Elly to show up. Yesterday and today I've been looking around for her.''

"Could she have gone back to the Stone house?'' Robin asked. "She liked it there, the pink room, and everything.''

Len shook his head. "I thought of that, but there's no way of getting in. We slammed the basement door when we left, so it locked.'' He went on eagerly. "Robin, *you* could do something. Call the Y.W.C.A. and places like that. *You'll* know what to say to them.''

"I can call some places, but I've got a better idea,'' Robin said. "We'll go and see Mr. Hill. He's a lawyer I met on the plane coming here. You'll like him—and he'll help you. I—I told him about you and Elly.''

Len shook his head. "He'll call the police!''

"No, he won't. He asked me to get you and Elly to see him, and he'd try to help you. You can tell him your story, Len. You'll like him.''

It took some time to make Len agree to see Mr. Hill, but at last he gave in. Robin went to the nearest telephone to call Mr. Hill's office. She kept her eye on Len, half afraid that he would run away. But he didn't, and when she came out he looked at her hopefully.

"He's out till half-past four, but we can see him then," Robin said.

"I'll meet you there," Len said. "I'll go back to Bill's place now and clean up."

"You didn't tell me about any Bill!"

"He's a kid I met in the park. A good kid," Len said. "He lives over on the West Side with his brother, and they let me sleep there last night."

"Oh, good," Robin said. She gave him Mr. Hill's address. "If you get there before me, go right on in—tell the girl in the office that Mr. Hill is expecting you." Feeling almost motherly, she added, "And Len, get yourself some rest and something to eat."

Robin went back to the apartment for lunch. When she had finished, she told May that she was going shopping and would be back in time for dinner.

Part of it was true. She would be home in time for dinner. But she wasn't going to do any shopping. She was going to do some looking. She was going to the brownstone house. She had a strange feeling that Elly was there—that, somehow, Elly had found a way in.

15

Robin waited until there was no one near the brownstone house. Then she went down the steps and tapped at the basement door. Softly at first, and then louder. She kept an eye on the window, thinking that Elly might peep out.

The door opened—but it was not Elly. A small, dark woman stood there. A woman in a black dress, with hair in a neat bun. Robin was too surprised to speak.

The woman looked her up and down. "Did you want something, miss?"

"I just—" Robin went red. She didn't know what to say. "Are the Stones living here again?"

"Not yet. They're staying in a hotel until the house is ready. I'm the housekeeper. Mrs. Stone is here this afternoon, to look things over. Do you want to see her?"

"Oh, no, thank you." Elly was not likely to be here, Robin thought. Not with people coming and going. "I—it doesn't matter, really."

As she turned to go, with the housekeeper

staring after her, a voice sounded. "Who is it, Anna? The telephone men?" A tall, slim woman came to the door. She was dressed in a pale gray suit and her hair was beautifully done.

She smiled at Robin. "I'm Mrs. Stone. Did they send you already? How quick they are!" Without waiting for an answer, she went on, "Come along in. We'll go upstairs to the breakfast room where we can talk."

Robin thought of running up the steps and away. But something stopped her. She might be able to find out if Elly had been back in the house. So she followed Mrs. Stone down the hallway and into the big kitchen.

"Do watch your step, Miss—er—" Mrs. Stone said. "Everything is so dusty. The house has been shut up for a long time."

"The kitchen isn't dusty, madam," Anna said. "That's funny, isn't it? It looks as if someone had cleaned it up a bit."

"How kind of them," Mrs. Stone said lightly. "More likely the windows have been shut so tightly that they kept the dust out."

Robin said nothing. Elly had cleaned up the kitchen, of course. But when?

Mrs. Stone led Robin upstairs and crossed a big hall to a small breakfast room. Here she took the dust covers off two chairs. "Sit down and let me look at you, my dear," she said.

Robin sat down. What was Mrs. Stone talking about, she wondered.

Mrs. Stone looked her up and down quickly, much as Anna had done. "You're a very pretty young lady," she said. "And I'm sure you're very bright. But surely you are much too young to be looking for a job."

"A job?" Robin shook her head. "I'm not looking for a job, Mrs. Stone. I've not even finished high school yet. And nobody sent me here. I mean I didn't come about—about *work*—" She stopped, startled. From above came a noise, a high, sharp noise that sounded like a scream.

Mrs. Stone jumped up. "Whatever was that? It sounded like a scream!"

"I think it came from upstairs," Robin said.

"Oh—upstairs!" To Robin's surprise, Mrs. Stone sat down again, smiling. "Then it's only Marie, my maid. She's a good girl but she's afraid of her own shadow." She made a funny little face. "When we were living in the country,

101

in France, poor Marie was afraid of everything—cows, pigs, even a little squirrel that got caught in her room."

Robin laughed. "Maybe she saw a mouse? I like mice myself, but a lot of girls I know scream when they see one."

"Perhaps we'd better go and see what's what?" Mrs. Stone said, getting up again. She went out into the big hall, Robin following her.

A wide staircase led up to the second floor. Mrs. Stone stood at the bottom and called up, "Marie! Marie, where are you?"

There was no answer. She called again. "Marie! Come down here, please!"

Again there was no answer. "Shall I run up and see where she is?" Robin asked. But as she started for the stairs, a young woman came out of one of the rooms on the second floor. She moved slowly down the stairs, her face white, her legs shaking.

"What is it this time, Marie?" Mrs. Stone said. "I never knew such a girl for getting scared!" She smiled. "Did you see a mouse?"

Marie opened her mouth but no words came.

Mrs. Stone spoke more gently. "Marie, whatever is the matter with you?"

"I saw a ghost, madam—a *ghost*. I heard a sound in Miss April's room and I looked in—"

"And saw a window cleaner!"

"No—no. I saw a ghost. It was lying in the bed. All white. And it—it was making a strange sound, like groaning."

"In Miss April's bed?" Mrs. Stone went pale, but she tried to smile. "Come now, Marie, you're imagining things."

"Of course she is!" Robin said quickly. "There's no such thing as ghosts." Her heart began to beat faster. *Elly*, she thought. It must be Elly in that room.

"But I *saw* it—in Miss April's room. In Miss April's bed," Marie was saying. "And I heard it cry out."

"Oh, Marie, do stop!" Robin said. Mrs. Stone, she saw, was very upset. She had put her hand on the stair rail to steady herself. "Look, Marie," Robin said. "Why don't you take Mrs. Stone back into the breakfast room where she can sit down. And I'll run upstairs and see what it is."

16

In April Stone's room, Robin moved quietly to the bed. Yes, it was Elly who lay there, white, thin, almost flat under the covers. Now and then her lips moved but Robin could not make out what she was saying.

"Elly," Robin said, bending over her. "Elly, it's me—Robin."

Elly turned her head from side to side. She looked at Robin with eyes that saw nothing. *She's ill,* Robin thought. She's very ill. I'll have to make them get her a doctor.

Gently, she pulled the covers up to Elly's chin and left the room, closing the door softly behind her.

In the breakfast room, Mrs. Stone started up from her chair as Robin came in. There was a little color in her face now. "Did you see anything? Is there really someone in the house?"

"Yes, there is—but of course it's not a ghost," Robin told her. "It's a young girl, and she's ill.

Her name is Elly but I don't know her last name."

"Elly?" Mrs. Stone frowned. "I don't know anyone named Elly—is she a friend of yours? Someone you know?"

Robin shook her head. "I wouldn't call her a friend. I've only seen her two or three times." Everything will have to come out now, she thought.

"But what is she doing in this house? Why is she in my daughter's room?" Mrs. Stone's hands were shaking again.

"She had nowhere to go. She's a runaway," Robin said. "I'll tell you everything I know about her, but it isn't much. But right now she's *ill*! Couldn't you please go up and look at her—"

Mrs. Stone pulled herself together. "Of course!" she said. As Robin started for the door, she shook her head. "No, you wait here, dear. If my husband comes in, tell him I'll be down soon."

In a few minutes, she was back again. "That little girl seems very ill," she said. "I'd like our doctor to see her—I'll call him." She started across the room, and stopped. "Oh, dear, I'd forgotten the telephone isn't working yet. Someone will have to go to the corner—"

She broke off as the door opened and a man came in. A man about sixty, with keen gray eyes. "I got here earlier than I expected, my dear," he told Mrs. Stone. Then he saw Robin. "I'm sorry. I guess you're busy with this young lady."

Mrs. Stone smiled faintly at Robin. "This is my husband," she said. "He'll take care of everything." She turned to the man. "Oh, John, I'm so glad you're here. Something very strange has been going on in the house! There's a young girl—a sick girl—in April's room. She's a runaway and she seems to have been hiding here."

"Mrs. Stone was just going to send for a doctor," Robin said. "I could go to the corner and telephone." She jumped up but Mr. Stone waved her back to her chair. "The car is still out in front," he said. "I'll send it for Doctor Black. He'll be finishing office hours now."

When he returned, he went quickly to his wife. "Are you all right, dear? You look very white."

"It was just the—the shock," Mrs. Stone said. "You see, Marie found the girl in April's bed, and she screamed so!"

"She would," Mr. Stone said. "And then?"

"Then this child ran upstairs and found the girl," Mrs. Stone said. She turned to Robin. "I don't even know why you came to see me—or your name or anything."

"It's a long story," Robin told them. "My name's Robin Green, and I'm staying with Judge Fox. She lives in the house across your back yard."

"Judge Fox, eh?" Mr. Stone nodded. "I've heard of her. A very fine woman."

"I've been visiting her while my parents are in France," Robin said. And the time is nearly over, she thought. Too bad.

"Now about this girl upstairs," Mr. Stone said. "Do I take it that you know her?"

"Not really," Robin said. "Perhaps I'd better begin at the beginning?"

Mrs. Stone smiled. "Yes, do that, dear. It may be a little while before Doctor Black gets here. But he'll come—he's an old friend of ours." She turned to Marie. "Marie, ask Anna to go upstairs and sit with that girl. Or you can sit with her yourself—there's nothing to be afraid of."

"Well, one night I was looking out of the

107

window," Robin began, "and I thought I saw dim lights moving about in your house. . . . "

She told them the whole story, though not about the monkey. That had nothing to do with the Stones, really. When she finished, Mr. Stone looked at his wife. "They don't seem to have done anything very terrible," he said.

"I honestly don't think they're bad kids at all," Robin said quickly. "Len was so worried that Elly would get sick. If we knew their whole story, maybe we wouldn't blame them—"

"Probably not," Mrs. Stone said. "But there's one thing I don't understand. What did Judge Fox make of all this?"

"Oh, she doesn't know anything about it!" Robin said. "I didn't tell her. I don't see much of her, for one thing. And—well, I guess I was afraid she'd have to go to the police."

Mr. Stone smiled at her. "It looks to me as if you're a young lady who likes to handle everything by herself," he said. He got up as steps sounded in the hall. "That will be Doctor Black. I suppose you'll want to go up with him, my dear?"

"Yes, I'll go," Mrs. Stone said. "You'd better see if you can get the telephone men to hurry—

you can call from the corner." At the door, she turned to speak to Robin. "Don't run away, dear. You'll want to hear what Doctor Black says."

When she came back, she was looking worried. "Elly will be all right," she said, "but she's a pretty sick little girl. Doctor Black says she has flu and is very run down—she isn't very strong."

"Are you sending her to the hospital?" Robin wanted to know.

"Yes. Doctor Black says that's the best place for her. He's going to send an ambulance." She frowned. "But we have to find out where Elly comes from. We'll have to get in touch with her parents."

"Len will know," Robin said. "I'm sure he'll tell us, now Elly is so ill—" She broke off with a little cry. "Oh, wow, I forgot all about Len!" She looked at her watch. "He's in Mr. Hill's office, waiting for me!"

17

Robin was upset. She hoped Len would not leave without seeing Mr. Hill. She had told him to go in without her, but you never knew!

"I'll have to run—Len's been waiting *ages* for me," Robin said. "I have to meet him at Mr. Hill's office—the lawyer I told you about."

"Jim will drive you over in the car," Mrs. Stone said, walking with Robin to the front door. "And I think we should all meet here tomorrow morning, say at eleven. You and Len—and Mr. Hill, too, if he can come." She smiled. "I rather think my husband may be able to do something for Len and Elly. But of course we'll want to know their full stories."

When Robin reached Mr. Hill's office, he and Len were just leaving. "We thought you'd run out on us," Mr. Hill said, smiling at her. "Let's go back into the office."

"I'm sorry to be so late," Robin said. "But—

well, I've found Elly, and the Stones are back. And they're so good!''

In the office, she told them how she had found Elly, ill. "Mr. Stone got a doctor, and Elly's going to the hospital. But Len, we have to know where Elly lives. They'll have to tell her parents about her.''

Len looked from Robin to Mr. Hill. "You're not going to believe this,'' he said, "but I don't know. Honest! Elly wouldn't tell me. She was afraid I would let her parents know where she was.''

"But where did you pick her up?'' Robin said. "You said you met her on a bus—where was it?''

Len shook his head. "I'd been on the bus half a day myself when Elly got on. Some little place. I wasn't taking any notice.''

"Perhaps if we looked at a road map,'' Mr. Hill said. He took one down from a bookcase, and Len opened it. Putting a finger on Kansas, Len began to trace a route. Suddenly he gave a cry. "Kansas City! I remember now. We were about half an hour out of Kansas City!''

He began to read off the names of small towns.

111

"Perry!" he said suddenly. "That's it! That's where Elly got on the bus. But I don't think she lives there. She said she'd hitched a ride there."

"It's a good place to start asking questions," Mr. Hill said. "I'll get in touch with the police there—and in Kansas City."

"Maybe you'll have found something out by tomorrow?" Robin said hopefully. "Mrs. Stone wants us all to meet there, at eleven. You, too, Mr. Hill, if you can come. I do hope you can!"

"I wouldn't miss it for anything." Mr. Hill smiled. "You two will have to run along now—I'm already late for an appointment." At the door, he said, "By the way, Robin, isn't it time you told Judge Fox everything that's been happening behind her back?"

Put that way, it sounded terrible. Robin went red. "I'll tell her tonight, I promise," she told him. "Len, can I drop you somewhere? Mr. Stone's car is waiting to take me home."

In the car, Len turned to Robin, frowning. "There's one thing that bugs me," he said. "How did Elly get into that house? We left everything

shut tight—and we locked the basement door behind us."

"I've no idea how she did it. When she's better, we'll ask her," Robin said. Elly, she thought, was very good at keeping secrets. Even from Len.

That evening, Judge Fox asked Robin if she would like to go to a movie. "No, thanks, not tonight," Robin said. She went pink. "If you don't have to go out, there's a long story I want to tell you. I—I hope you won't think I've behaved badly when you hear it."

"Behaved *badly*?" Judge Fox looked at her in surprise. "That would certainly surprise me, Robin. You've been a wonderful guest, no trouble at all. I'm only sorry I haven't been able to spend more time with you."

"That's one reason I didn't want to bother you. You always looked so tired when you got home."

Supper over, they settled down in the living room. Robin told her story well and clearly, and Judge Fox listened, asking a question now and then. Suddenly she smiled. "I can quite under-

114

stand why you didn't tell me," she said. "After all, I'm a judge. I might have thought it my duty to turn those young people over to the police."

"I know," Robin said. "And they're not bad kids, really. Elly is so easily scared. But Len's brave, and he has plenty of sense. I'm sure he must have had some good reason for leaving home."

"The Stones seem to see things your way," Judge Fox said. "I wish I could be with you when you all meet in the morning—but of course you'll tell me all about it."

"Oh, I will," Robin said. "And I *do* want to thank you for being so understanding. You've been so kind, and I've had such a good time here."

"A different sort of time, anyway," Judge Fox said. "Wait till May hears all this! Are you going to tell her?"

"Oh, yes, I will before I leave," Robin said. "I didn't dare tell her before. You know May—she'd never have let me out of the apartment if she knew what I was up to!"

18

Robin was so eager to get to the brownstone house next day that she was half an hour early. She walked around the block until Mr. Hill and Len arrived, right on time.

"Hi, Mr. Hill. Hi, Len!" She hurried up to them. "It seems funny to be going into this house by the front door!"

Len laughed. "Saves wall climbing," Mr. Hill said. They went up the front steps and rang the bell.

Mrs. Stone herself answered and led them into a pretty little sitting room. Robin presented Mr. Hill. "And this is Len," she said. "He can tell you his last name."

"Len Pond." He shook hands shyly with Mrs. Stone. "Ma'am, I hope you'll forgive us for hiding in your house. We didn't exactly break in—though maybe Elly did this time. I don't know how she got in again!"

"I do," Mrs. Stone said. "Suppose we all sit

116

down and I'll tell you." When they were settled, she went on, "You see, I found Elly's bag near the bed—and *this* was in it." She held up a key.

They all stared at it. "The key to the basement door," Len said. "She must have taken it. I thought she'd left it on its hook, as I told her!" He looked at Mrs. Stone. "I guess she wanted to sleep in a real bed. She isn't strong, and she kept getting colds."

Mrs. Stone smiled at him. "It was good of you to look after her, Len. I'm sure things would have been easier for you on your own."

"Maybe—but I couldn't leave her. Things were not so hard for me. I have no folks to worry about—or to worry about *me*. I—" He looked at Mr. Hill. "You tell them, sir."

"Len's parents died when he was ten," Mr. Hill said. "And he grew up in many homes. Usually he was put with farm people—and he doesn't want to be a farmer. He wanted to go East and get more schooling. He thought he might even be able to get to college some day."

"And why not?" Mrs. Stone said gently. "My husband and I have been talking about this.

117

Perhaps we can help Len. Because we have no son of our own to help any more." She turned to Len. "We'd like Mr. Hill to take charge of things—let the people in your hometown know that you're safe. And that we will keep an eye on you in the future." She smiled. "It won't be hard to find a room for you, and get you back to school."

Len found it hard to speak. "That sounds fine, ma'am. I don't know how to thank you." He did not look as happy as Robin expected and she thought she knew why. "But it's Elly I'm worried about," he said. "The city's no place for her. She's a country girl, and she doesn't really want to live anywhere else. But she says she won't go back home—and she won't tell me why."

"We'll find out, in time," Mr. Hill said. "At least we know she doesn't come from Perry. I've found that much out. I've yet to hear from Missing Persons in Kansas City."

"For the time being, Elly's safe in the hospital," Mrs. Stone said. "I telephoned this morning, and you'll be able to see her soon. Perhaps tomorrow."

118

"I can't tomorrow, much as I'd like to," Robin said. "Ann—Judge Fox—has one of her few free days, and we're going to spend it together."

Robin and Len turned to leave, but Mr. Hill stayed behind to talk with Mrs. Stone. "My husband will be here soon," Robin heard her say, "and I know he wants to talk with you about the two youngsters. It will be good for him to have something to think about. Coming back to this house has been sad for us—but it's home, and we both want to make our lives here again."

In the street, Len said to Robin, "I'll sure be glad if Mrs. Stone can find me a room. I can't stay much longer at Bill's place—they need the couch. And I—" he gave her a funny little smile, "well, I don't really get any kick out of sleeping in the subway!"

Judge Fox had invited Len to have dinner with them that night. The more Robin saw of him, the more she liked him. Judge Fox, too, found a lot to like in him. "There's nothing wrong with that boy," she said. "He says very little about the homes he has lived in—which means he hasn't been happy. But he knows where he wants to go—and he'll get there. He's clever, and he seems very sensible."

Two days later, Robin had lunch with Mrs. Stone. The house was almost ready for its owners. The dust covers had been taken off. The windows shone. There were flowers everywhere.

After lunch, they went to see Elly. Robin was allowed in the room for five minutes. "Because she's still very weak," the nurse said.

This time, when Elly opened her eyes, she smiled at Robin and said "Hi" in a small voice. Robin told her that Len was fine and was getting a room, and Elly's eyes shone. "Len's so good," she said softly. *"Everyone's* so good to me."

The nurse told Mrs. Stone that Elly had spoken very little and had said nothing about who she was or where she came from.

Late the next evening, Len rang the bell of Judge Fox's apartment. When Robin answered the door, he gave her a broad smile. "I just stopped by to tell you I'm all set. I'm going to stay in Brooklyn with Jim's family!"

"The man who drives for the Stones? Oh, *good!"*

"I'm on my way there now." Len showed her a worn old bag. "With all my worldly goods!" He went with Robin into the living room. "Jim's only charging me a few bucks for my room, and the Stones are going to give me some jobs to do. They want to fix up their yard again and I'm pretty good at that kind of work." He drew an excited breath. "I've been dreaming, too. One more year of school and then—well, I'm going to see if there's any way I can get to college."

"You'll get there," Robin told him. "I have a feeling the Stones will help you."

"It's thanks to *you,* Robin. You've done it all, really. If you hadn't come peeping into the windows of the Stone house—"

"And if you hadn't grabbed me and pulled me in!" Robin laughed. "That rough stuff really scared me—but I wasn't going to show it!"

They were laughing and talking when May called to Robin. "There's a gentleman here asking for you, Robin. He says you know him. His name is Hill, and there's another gentleman with him."

19

Robin jumped up and went to meet the men.
"Oh, Mr. Hill, how nice! Do come in," she said.
"Len's here, and we've been talking our heads
off." She glanced at the man who was with him.
He was taller and older than Mr. Hill, with sun-
burned hair and a weather-beaten face."

"Hi, there, Len," Mr. Hill said, as the two men
came into the living room. "I've brought someone I'm sure you'll like to meet. You, too, Robin."
He put his hand on the other man's arm. "This is
Mr. West, Elly's father."

"Elly's father!" Robin looked up into a pair of
friendly gray eyes. Why ever would Elly run away
from a father like this? He looked so nice, with
such a warm smile.

"He flew in from Kansas City a few hours ago,
and we've been at the Stone house since then,"
Mr. Hill said. "And at the hospital."

"Did you see Elly—how is she?" Robin wanted
to know.

"She's doing well, they say. The nurse let me

talk to her for fifteen minutes," Elly's father said. "Time enough to straighten out a lot of things."

"Are you going to take her home with you?" That was Len. To Robin's surprise his voice was sharp, his face dark.

"Mr. Stone will put her on a plane when she's fit to fly," Mr. Hill said. "That'll be in ten days or so. Mr. West has to get back to his farm—"

"And my two little sons," Mr. West added. "They've been running wild since Elly left us. They miss her badly. She's been a real mother to them since my wife died, four years ago."

"Why did Elly run away?" Len asked, his eyes hard. "Kids don't run away from home if they're happy!"

Mr. West's smile faded. "I guess you've a right to know," he said. "From all I hear, you've taken good care of Elly since you two met—and I want to thank you." He frowned. "Elly had her reasons for running away. She knew I was planning to get married again, and she didn't like Candy, the young woman I was seeing. Didn't trust her, either. And she was right. Just after Elly left home, Candy and the cashier where she worked stole a large sum of money—and ran off together." He laughed shortly. "End of love story! Now all I want is to get my girl home—and Elly wants it, too."

They talked for more than an hour after that. Elly's father described their farm in Oak Corners, Kansas, and how Elly loved the life there. "We'll soon have her strong and bossing us all again. Plenty of good milk, and fresh eggs and butter."

He wanted to know what was in store for Len, and Len told him he meant to finish high school and then try to go to college.

"You deserve to," Mr. West said. "You're a good lad. We—Elly and I—hope you'll keep in touch with us—maybe come and visit."

It was Mr. Hill who brought the talk to an end. "Too bad to break this up, but I have to get Mr. West to a hotel," he said. "He has to catch a plane early in the morning."

Len left with them. "I'll see you again before you leave, won't I?" he asked Robin. "How much longer have you got?"

"Three days!" Robin said. She couldn't believe how the time had flown.

20

For Robin, the next three days passed in a whirl. She had Len for company, except when Mr. Stone carried him off to shop for clothes or for things he would need for school in the Fall. "They're doing too much for me," Len said, worried. "I'll never be able to pay them back. All I've done for them so far is some planting in their yard."

"They don't want you to do anything," Robin said. "They're really doing it for their son. They said that. Besides, they *like* you!"

Together, Robin and Len saw some of the "sights" they had missed up to now, like the United Nations Building. They took the bus uptown to The Cloisters, high on a hill above the Hudson River. In the court-yards, they took pictures of each other under trees and by fountains. "I've got so used to you, Len," Robin said. "I'm going to miss you! How are you at writing letters?"

125

Len laughed. "How should *I* know? I've never had anyone to write to. I can put sentences together—and spell, if that's what you mean." He was suddenly serious. "I'll write to you, Robin. That's a promise."

But would he, Robin wondered. Most boys hated writing letters. Perhaps Len was different. She hoped so.

The day before Robin left, the Stones gave her a farewell party. Judge Fox and Mr. Hill were invited, too. And Len, of course. Elly was still in the hospital, but Robin and Len told her all about it later.

They went to a Japanese place on Park Avenue. Robin and Len ate in the Japanese way, sitting on mats on the floor. The older people, mindful of their bones, sat at a table.

As they ate, Robin suddenly remembered the dinner she had thought she would go to with Ricky, the boy she had dreamed up. She decided she liked Len better. He was stronger, more of a man, than the Ricky of her silly dreams.

When they were nearly at the end of their meal, Mrs. Stone spoke to her from the table.

126

"We've just been saying that you must come and visit New York again, Robin. Elly, too, if she can."

"Oh, I'd love it!" Robin said. She smiled at Judge Fox. "That is, if Ann will have me."

"I will—if you bring your mother," Judge Fox said.

"Oh, Robin must stay with us too," Mr. Stone said. "We'd love to see her again."

"But no more breaking into dark houses," Judge Fox said. "Next time you might not be so lucky!"

And Robin agreed.

About the Author

NORAH SMARIDGE is the daughter of a sea captain and comes from a long line of seafolk from Devonshire, England. After taking an Honors degree at London University, she came to New York and took writing courses at Columbia and Hunter.

Although she has been writing since she was nine, the author has had various occupations. She taught for ten years, then worked in a bookstore, a literary agency, and as a copywriter.

Now writing full time, Miss Smaridge is at her desk from nine to three, and she says it is work—but she loves it! She types everything, and has produced light verse, serials, short stories, TV scripts, newspaper articles and columns, and many books. She writes mainly for children, young people, and seniors.

A resident of Upper Montclair, New Jersey, Norah Smaridge has lots of young neighbors—and far too many cats. She enjoys traveling and mild gardening, and is an omnivorous reader.

About the Artist

MICHAEL HAMPSHIRE, illustrator of many books and magazines, grew up on Yorkshire's moors. An amateur archaeologist, he settled in New York City after traveling extensively in Africa and the East.